THOSE 11 DOORWAYS

11 KEY IDEAS FOR LIFE

SHIVAM DWIVEDI

Made with ♥ on the Notion Press Platform
www.notionpress.com

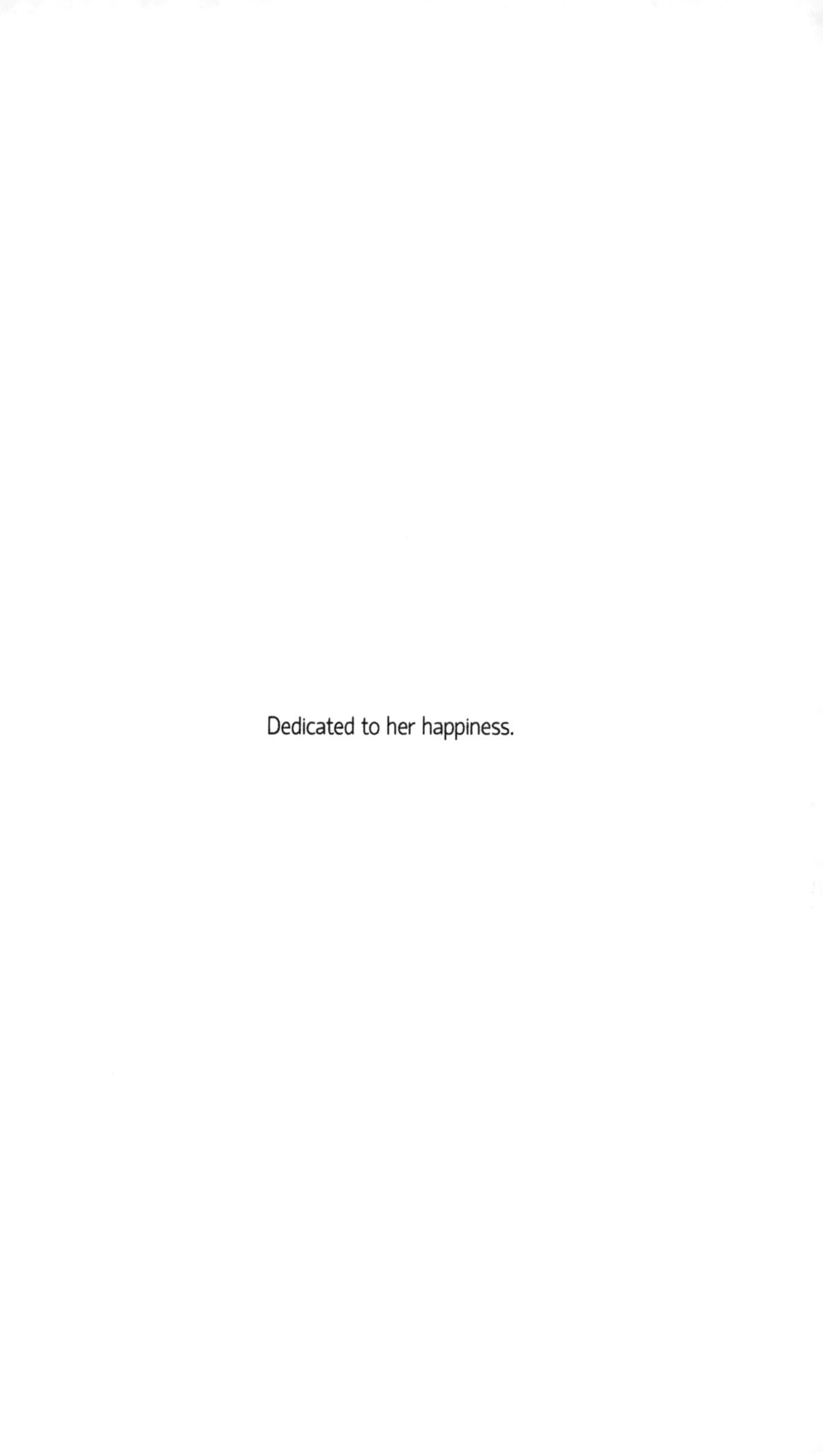

Dedicated to her happiness.

Contents

Foreword

In this inspiring novel, we follow the story of two brothers, Joshwa and Satyam, as they navigate the complexities of life and the challenges that come with it.

Through a simple yet meaningful gift, Joshwa shares his personal lessons and insights with his brother, Satyam.

Lessons that have been hard-won through his own life experiences and many hours of reading and learning. And as Satyam begins to read through the booklet, he realizes the value of his brother's gift and how it could impact his life.

This story is about the power of brotherhood, the importance of mentorship, and the transformative impact that simple acts of kindness and sharing can have on our lives.

We follow the journey of these two brothers as they explore what it means to be successful, happy, and fulfilled in life, and how we can all benefit from the wisdom and guidance of those who have come before us.

As you embark on this journey, I hope you find inspiration and insight in the lessons shared by Joshwa and Satyam, and that you too can learn to navigate the complex landscape of life with courage and purpose.

Preface

Joshwa and Satyam were two brothers, each on their own journey through life. Joshwa, the elder of the two, had always felt a strong sense of responsibility to guide and protect his younger brother.

Although their bond was not always perfect, Joshwa knew that he wanted to be there for Satyam and help him to succeed.

It was on a lazy Sunday afternoon that Joshwa decided to share with Satyam some of the lessons he had learned over the years.

He pulled out a small booklet that he had put together, filled with the knowledge and wisdom he had gleaned from his experiences and the books he had read.

As Satyam began to read through the pages, he realized that his brother had much to teach him.

In this story, we follow the journey of Joshwa and Satyam as they navigate the twists and turns of life, relying on each other for support and guidance. Through Joshwa's lessons, we gain insight into the challenges and triumphs of growing up, and the importance of family and personal growth.

Acknowledgements

Dreams

Prologue

As Satyam read through the booklet that his elder brother Joshwa had given him, he feels a sense of wonder and curiosity. He had always known that his brother was wise and insightful, but he had never realized just how much he had learned over the years.

With each passing page, Satyam felt as though he was gaining a new perspective on life.

The lessons in the booklet were not just practical, they were also deeply philosophical, delving into the fundamental questions of what it means to be alive and how we can find meaning and purpose in a complex and often confusing world.

As he finished the last page, Satyam looked up at his brother, feeling a newfound sense of admiration and respect.

He realized that Joshwa had not just been trying to protect him all these years, he had also been preparing him for the challenges and opportunities that lay ahead.

With a new sense of purpose and determination, Satyam knew that he was ready to take on whatever life had in store for him. And he was grateful to have an elder brother like Joshwa to guide him along the way.

That Special Sunday

Joshwa have always been protective of his younger brother, Satyam.

As they grew up, Joshwa felt a sense of responsibility to guide Satyam and help him navigate the ups and downs of life. He wanted Satyam to be happy and successful, and he knew that he had a role to play in making that happen. Their bonding was not quite good though.

On one Sunday, as they sat together on the porch, Joshwa decided to have a heart-to-heart conversation with Satyam. He wanted to share some of the lessons he had learned over the years and help Satyam avoid some of the mistakes he had made.

Satyam! I hope you don't have any special plan today.

What do you want Jo? It is Sunday today. Just let me have a break. It is my special day, too.

Joshwa: Come on, Sit here, I have something I would like to show you.

Satyam: What is this ...11 doorways?

Joshwa: It's my booklet. This is something what I have learnt so far in my life, by reading several books and experiencing different circumstances. Maybe you feel silly or weird about it at first but trust me, it is going to help you in your life.

I have more, I want to share with my brother but first please have a look into this and I am sure it will definitely benefit you.

Joshwa passes him the booklet and he starts reading it from lesson 1.

CHAPTER ONE

But

There are instances when we need to criticize or correct others. Always start this process with sincere and honest praise.

The problem then occurs when we follow that praise with the dreaded word "But".

For example, "I've got to say bro, you're looking muscular, but your legs look skinny."

So, what started as really nice praise totally collapsed by using the word "but".

The good news is with some minor tweaking, these same words can be said without any negative consequence. All we have to do is replace the word 'but' with and tweak the last sentence. We could say, "I've got to say bro, you're looking muscular, and if you work your legs a bit more, it will be perfect!"

CHAPTER TWO

Power of Constraint

The power of constraint refers to the idea that limitations can actually enhance creativity and problem-solving abilities. Constraints force us to think more creatively, as we are forced to work within a set of boundaries or limitations.

This can lead to unexpected solutions and innovative ideas that we may not have otherwise considered.

For example, a graphic designer may be asked to create a logo using only two colors and a specific font.

The constraints of the project force the designer to think more creatively, exploring different combinations and layouts to create a logo that is both unique and effective.

The power of constraint demonstrates that limitations can be beneficial for creativity and problem-solving, as they force us to think more creatively and work within a set of boundaries to find innovative solutions. By embracing constraints, we can unlock new possibilities and achieve better results.

CHAPTER THREE

Spending Habits

I am committed to spending my money wisely, ensuring that I save enough to achieve my long-term goals. While I strive to be frugal, I also understand the importance of not being too stingy. Thanks to the valuable insights I've gained from various books on money management, such as "21 Laws of Money", I have developed a framework for optimizing my spending habits.

Whenever I consider spending a rupee, I ask myself one crucial question: "Will this cash outflow enhance my health, relationships, knowledge, or wealth?" If the answer is a heartfelt "yes", I happily spend the money.

For example, spending on fruits to improve my health is a wise choice, while spending money on pizza is not. Buying a gift for someone can enhance my relationships, while investing in books, e-courses, and seminars can improve my knowledge. Similarly, investing in my start-up idea can add to my wealth in the long run.

By adopting this approach, I ensure that every rupee I spend aligns with my long-term goals and helps me make progress towards achieving them.

CHAPTER FOUR

Expectation Adjustment

Expectations play a critical role in our happiness and motivation.

For example: The experience of a hungry teenager in a poor country is far different from that of a perfectionist student in a developed country who might become depressed for weeks after receiving a "B" in school. In contrast, a student who expects to fail would be ecstatic to receive a "B."

To experience greater happiness, we can adjust our expectations and appreciate what we do have rather than focusing on what we lack. Doing so can help us manage disappointment, concentrate on achievable goals, and foster personal growth.

Learning to adjust our expectations is an essential skill that enables us to navigate the ups and downs of life.

By reassessing our expectations and modifying them when necessary, we become more adaptable, resilient, and successful in achieving our goals.

CHAPTER FIVE

Someday Syndrome

Many young graduates take on demanding jobs at high-powered firms with the intention of working hard to earn enough money to retire and pursue their true interests by age 35.

However, by the time they reach that age, they have accumulated significant financial obligations, including large home loans, schooling costs for their children, credit card bills, and expenses associated with suburban living.

They may also feel that life is not worth living without indulging in high-end luxuries like fine wine and exotic vacations.

In this situation, it's easy to feel trapped and wonder if there is any way out. Some may question whether they should give up their high-powered jobs and go back to their previous work, but this may not be a feasible option for many.

Instead, people often double down and work even harder in the hope that they will someday be able to work on their passion. However, this kind of thinking can lead to a perpetual state of delay and missed opportunities.

In fact, the majority of people experience what is often referred to as the "Someday Syndrome," where they continually put off their dreams and goals until some unspecified future date.

However, there are ways to break out of this cycle and start making progress toward your goals.

By taking small steps, setting achievable targets, and being consistent in your efforts, you can start building the life you want today. Instead of waiting for "someday," take action now and start living the life you truly desire.

CHAPTER SIX

Small Wins

It's often said that life is better when we have small wins every day rather than waiting for one big win in the future.

By breaking down our goals into smaller, achievable steps, we create a consistent feedback loop of small wins that keeps us motivated.

Our subconscious mind doesn't differentiate between big and small achievements, only between success and failure. So, it's the frequency of our wins that motivates us, not the size of the win.

For instance, if our goal is to finish a 200-page book, it can take a month or longer to achieve that goal.

However, if we break the goal down into smaller tasks like reading six pages a day, we can achieve a win every day. This provides almost 30 positive feedbacks to the subconscious mind in a month.

In summary, breaking down our goals into smaller, achievable steps is a powerful way to create a consistent feedback loop of small wins that keeps us motivated and helps us achieve our goals.

CHAPTER SEVEN

Embrace Introverts

Did you know that as much as one-third to one-half of the population are introverts?

That means that one out of every two or three people you know is likely to be an introvert. Unfortunately, many introverts hide even from themselves, and it is a mistake to embrace the "Extrovert is best" principle.

It's important to recognize that without introverts, we wouldn't have many of the great inventions and works of art that we enjoy today, such as the theory of gravity, the theory of relativity, Charlie Brown, Google, and Harry Potter. Neither $E=mc^2$ nor Paradise Lost was produced by a party animal.

This shows that the quality of an idea has zero correlation to the ability to express it. Yet, the ideas of talkative people are often assumed to be the best.

In order to embrace introverts, it's essential to create an environment that accommodates their needs and preferences.

This may include providing quiet spaces for reflection or reducing the amount of stimulation in a given environment. By valuing and respecting the unique strengths and needs of introverts, we can create a more inclusive and supportive community for all individuals.

CHAPTER EIGHT

Authentic Happiness

There is a common question about whether happiness comes from having fun or from the exercise of kindness. To find out, a classroom was asked to engage in one pleasurable activity and one philanthropic activity.

The results were life-changing as the afterflow of the pleasurable activity paled against the effects of the kind action.

For example, when you offer food or money to a homeless person, you are doing something kind for someone else, which may give you a sense of purpose and connection to others.

The act of kindness may also be reciprocated in some way, such as a smile or a thank you, which can make you feel good about your actions.

Over time, these small acts of kindness can add up and make you feel happier and more fulfilled in your life.

The exercise of kindness is a gratification that calls on your strengths to rise to an occasion and meet a challenge. It may not have positive emotions like joy, but it consists of total engagement and the loss of self-consciousness.

CHAPTER NINE

Performer & Learner

There are two types of people in the world: those who view life as a performance and those who view it as a work in progress.

Performers are primarily focused on achieving a specific goal or outcome, such as winning a competition or delivering a successful performance.

On the other hand, learners are actively seeking to acquire new knowledge or skills and are more focused on understanding and developing their abilities.

Ironically, our educational system is designed to produce performers, not learners.

The emphasis is often placed on successful performance rather than successful learning, and there are typically penalties for failure and rewards for accomplishment, as if failure and learning are separate entities.

In contrast, a learner is open to making mistakes and is willing to experiment in order to improve. They may struggle initially but are dedicated to understanding the material and developing their skills.

Moreover, when it is safe to talk about mistakes, individuals are more likely to report errors and less likely to make them.

Performers and learners can create a dynamic and innovative environment that can lead to continued growth and development when they work together.

CHAPTER TEN

Action & Motivation

The relationship between motivation and action is a complex one, and it is not always clear which comes first.

Motivation can cause action in several ways. For example, when we are motivated to achieve a goal or pursue a particular interest, we may be more likely to take action towards that goal or interest.

On the other hand, action can also cause motivation. When we take action towards a goal, we may experience a sense of progress or accomplishment that can further motivate us to continue pursuing that goal.

Additionally, taking action can also help us build confidence and overcome obstacles that may have previously held us back.

It is important to recognize that motivation and action are interconnected, and both are important for achieving our goals and pursuing our interests. While motivation can inspire us to take action, taking action can also help us build motivation and momentum towards achieving our desired outcomes.

CHAPTER ELEVEN

Being Creative

Creativity is the ability to generate new and original ideas, concepts, or solutions to problems. It is not just limited to artistic expression, but it can be applied to any area of life, from business and technology to education and personal growth.

Being creative requires an open and curious mind, a willingness to take risks, and the ability to think outside the box. It involves exploring new perspectives, experimenting with different approaches, and embracing uncertainty and ambiguity.

Creative individuals often have a natural curiosity and a passion for learning. They are not afraid to ask questions, challenge assumptions, and explore different ideas. They are also able to see things from multiple angles and consider a range of possibilities.

Being creative can be incredibly rewarding, both personally and professionally. It can lead to innovative ideas, breakthroughs, and solutions that can have a profound impact on the world. It can also bring a sense of fulfillment and purpose to one's life.

By embracing our creative potential, we can unlock new opportunities, challenge old ways of thinking, and create a brighter future for ourselves and the world.

Best Birthday Gift

After finishing the booklet, Satyam sat with the book in his hands, taking in the words and ideas that his elder brother had gifted him for his birthday. He couldn't help but feel grateful for the unexpected & best present, and he knew he had to show his appreciation.

Later that day, the Satyam sat down to write a heartfelt letter to his Joshwa. He expressed his gratitude for the thoughtful gift and shared how much he enjoyed reading the book.

He also talked about the insights he had gained from the book and how it had inspired him to think differently about his own life.

When he finished writing the letter, he sealed it in an envelope and left it on his Joshwa's desk.

Later, when Joshwa read the letter, he couldn't help but feel a sense of pride and joy in knowing that his gift had been so well-received. The younger brother's thoughtful words served as a reminder of the special bond they shared, and the elder brother was filled with a sense of warmth and love.

About The Author

Shivam Dwivedi is a multifaceted personality with a passion for helping others. As a Personality Development Coach, Educator, Writer, Freelancer, and Social Worker, Shivam has made it his mission to enhance the lives of young people.

Despite coming from a commerce background, Shivam's thirst for knowledge has driven him to explore areas outside his comfort zone. His areas of expertise range from culture and languages to philosophy and personal development.

A voracious reader and a passionate learner, Shivam has dedicated his life to improving the lives and wellbeing of young people.

He started his journey as a counselor for a few young students and has now expanded his work to include promoting our true Indian culture through his association with the Trust "Saptrishikulam."

Shivam's coaching and mentoring approach is tailored to the individual's unique needs and goals, and he strongly believes in helping young people find their true purpose in life.

With his vast knowledge and experience, Shivam has become a trusted mentor for many, and his commitment to helping others is nothing short of inspiring.

Whether you're struggling to find direction in life or seeking to improve your personal and professional growth, Shivam Dwivedi is the coach for you. Join the ranks of many who have benefited from his guidance and support and take the first step towards a better, more fulfilling life.

9 798889 758075

Printed by Libri Plureos GmbH in Hamburg,
Germany